THE ANIMAL FAIR

Animal verses compiled by
JILL BENNETT

Illustrated by
SUSIE JENKIN-PEARCE

VIKING

For Poppy (Pawanjit) (JB)
For Trisha (SJP)

VIKING

Published by the Penguin Group
27 Wrights Lane, London W8 5TZ, England
Viking Penguin Inc., 40 West 23rd Street, New York, New York 10010, USA
Penguin Books Australia Ltd, Ringwood, Victoria, Australia
Penguin Books Canada Ltd, 2801 John Street, Markham, Ontario, Canada L3R 1B4
Penguin Books (NZ) Ltd, 182–190 Wairau Road, Auckland 10, New Zealand

Penguin Books Ltd, Registered Offices: Harmondsworth, Middlesex, England

First published 1990
10 9 8 7 6 5 4 3 2 1

This selection copyright © Jill Bennett, 1990
Illustrations copyright © Susie Jenkin-Pearce, 1990

Typeset in Linotron 202 Baskerville by
Rowland Phototypesetting (London) Ltd
Printed in Hong Kong by Longmans

A CIP catalogue record for this book is available from the British Library

ISBN 0–670–82691–X

The Furry Ones

I like –
the furry ones –
the waggy ones
the purry ones
the hoppy ones
that hurry,

The glossy ones
the saucy ones
the sleepy ones
the leapy ones
the mousy ones
that scurry,

The snuggly ones
the huggly ones
the never, never
ugly ones…
all soft
and warm
and furry.

Aileen Fisher

Farmyard

Little hen
feathered and red
pecking round for scraps of bread.

Little goat
fierce and white
thinks his rope is much too tight.

Little calf
soft and shy
peeking out with one brown eye.

Little cat
black and lean
crouching so he won't be seen.

Little pig
muddy and stout
trying hard to wriggle out.

Gail Gregory

Snail

Little snail,
Dreaming you go.
Weather and rose
Is all you know.

Weather and rose
Is all you see,
Drinking
The dewdrops
Mystery.

Langston Hughes

Caterpillar

Creepy crawly caterpillar
Looping up and down,
Furry tufts of hair along
Your back of golden brown.

You will soon be wrapped in silk,
Asleep for many a day;
And then, a handsome butterfly,
You'll stretch and fly away.

Mary Dawson

If I Had A Pony

If I had a pony
with a coat of velvet black,
I'd lead him out of winter
and leap upon his back.

I'd ride him down a meadow
and through a stretch of pine –
a cloud would make a shadow,
the sun would make a shine.

The air would smell of rainbows
and robin-birds would sing,
and I would tell my pony,
'It's spring today. It's SPRING.'

Aileen Fisher

A Dragon-fly

When the heat of the summer
Made drowsy the land,
A dragon-fly came
And sat on my hand,
With its blue jointed body,
And wings like spun glass,
It lit on my fingers
As though they were grass.

Eleanor Farjeon

Wasps

Wasps in brightly
Coloured vests,
Chewing wood,
To make their nests.

Wasps, like rockets,
Zooming high,
Then dropping down
Where peaches lie.

Anne Ruddick

Animal Fair

I went to the animal fair,
All the birds and beasts were there,
The big baboon by the light of the moon
Was combing his auburn hair.
The monkey fell from his bunk
And slid down the elephant's trunk.
The elephant sneezed, and fell on his knees
And what became of the mon-key,
     mon-key, mon-key, mon-key,
     monkey, monk.

Anon.

Honey Bear

There was a big bear
Who lived in a cave;
His greatest love
Was honey.
He had twopence a week
Which he never could save,
So he never had
Any money.
I bought him a money-box
Red and round,
In which to put
His money.
He saved and saved
Till he got a pound,
Then he spent it all
On honey.

Elizabeth Lang

Pets

I'm a dog
All tail and bark,
Snapping, yapping
In the park.

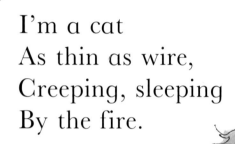

I'm a cat
As thin as wire,
Creeping, sleeping
By the fire.

I'm a rabbit
All fluff and ear,
Trapped in a cage
And twitching fear.

John Kitching

Five Little Pussy Cats

Five little pussy cats playing near the door;
        One ran and hid inside
        And then there were four.

Four little pussy cats underneath a tree;
        One heard a dog bark
        And then there were three.

Three little pussy cats thinking what to do;
        One saw a little bird
        And then there were two.

Two little pussy cats sitting in the sun;
        One ran to catch his tail
        And then there was one.

One little pussy cat looking for some fun;
        He saw a butterfly –
        And then there was none.

Anon.

Slide-Swim-Fly

Snake slide slip slither
Over hard dry clay.
Snake slide slip slither
Hot hot day.

Fish swim swish sway
Through the murky way.
Fish swim swish sway
Deep deep bay.

Bird fly flutter flit
Through the open sky.
Bird fly flutter flit
Blue blue sky.

Sue Cochrane

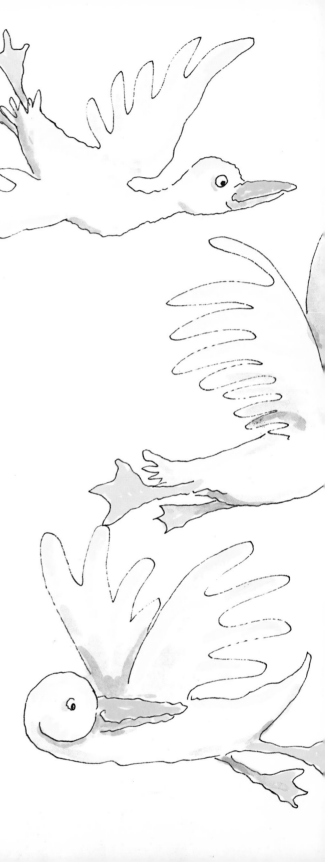

A Little Cock Sparrow

A little cock sparrow sat on a green tree,
And he chirruped, he chirruped, so merry was he.
A naughty boy came with his wee bow and arrow,
Says he, I will shoot this little cock sparrow.
His body will make me a nice little stew,
And his giblets will make me a little pie too.
Oh, no, said the sparrow, I won't make a stew,
So he clapped his wings and away he flew.

Anon.

Here Is The Ostrich

Here is the ostrich straight and tall,
Nodding his head above us all.

Here is the long snake on the ground,
Wriggling on the stones around.

Here are the birds that fly so high,
Spreading their wings across the sky.

Here is the bushrat, furry and small,
Rolling himself into a ball.

Here is the spider scuttling round,
Treading so lightly on the ground.

Here are the children fast asleep,

And here at night the owls do peep.

Anon.

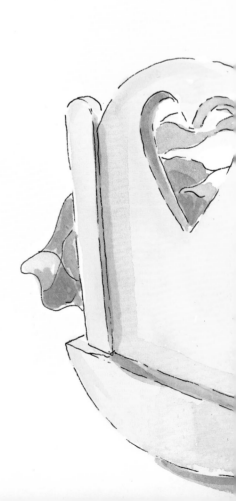

The Kangaroo

Old Jumpety-Bumpety-Hop-and-Go-One
Was lying asleep on his side in the sun.
This old kangaroo, he was whisking the flies
(With his long glossy tail) from his ears and his eyes.
Jumpety-Bumpety-Hop-and-Go-One
Was lying asleep on his side in the sun,
Jumpety-Bumpety-Hop!

Anon.

If You Should Meet A Crocodile

If you should meet a crocodile,
    Don't take a stick and poke him;
Ignore the welcome in his smile,
    Be careful not to stroke him.
For as he sleeps upon the Nile,
    He thinner gets and thinner;
And whene'er you meet a crocodile
    He's ready for his dinner.

Anon.

A Zoo Party

I'd like to give a party
And ask them all to tea;
The alligator, antelope,
The owl and chimpanzee;
The elephant and eagle;
The fox and the gazelle;
The tiger and the llama;
The octopus and snail;
The python and the pelican.
I'd ask them all to come,
And, of course, I'd have the penguins
Or it wouldn't be such fun.

I'd have the lion cubs for sure.
I must have polar bears.
I'd like to have a walrus,
And the wild cat – if she cares;
I'd have – but, when I think of it,
What would we have to eat?
And I wouldn't like the tiger
To come and share *my* seat.
It scarcely would be pleasant,
To say the very least,
To give the zoo a party
And find *I* was the feast.

Alexander Reid

The Leopard

The leopard creeps quietly,
Creeps in the night,
Creeps when the stars
And the moon are bright.

The leopard creeps softly,
Up on the hill,
Peeps from the bushes,
Waiting to kill.

Anon.

The Lion Roars With A Fearful Sound

The lion roars with a fearful sound,
    Roar, roar, roar!

The lion creeps, its prey to catch,
    Creep, creep, creep!

The lion pounces with a mighty leap,
    Leap, leap, leap!

The lion eats with a crunching sound,
    Crunch, crunch, crunch!

The lion sleeps with a gentle snore,
    Snore, snore, snore!

Mabel Segun

Three Mice

Three little mice walked into town,
Their coats were grey, and their eyes were brown.

Three little mice went down the street,
With woolwork slippers upon their feet.

Three little mice sat down to dine
On curranty bread and gooseberry wine.

Three little mice ate on and on,
Till every crumb of the bread was gone.

Three little mice, when the feast was done,
Crept home quietly one by one.

Three little mice went straight to bed,
And dreamt of crumbly, curranty bread.

Charlotte Druitt Cole

Night Out

Nobody knows
where Tim-cat goes.
Down the road? Or through the meadow?

Into the night
and out of sight
he hurries past the purple shadow.

At break of day
he's back to stay,
contented with our sunny dwelling.

But nobody knows
where Tim-cat goes
at night ... and Tim-cat isn't telling.

Aileen Fisher

Dormouse

'Now Winter is coming,'
The dormouse said,
'I must be thinking
Of going to bed.'
So he curled himself up
As small as he could,
And went fast asleep
As a dormouse should.

Lilian McCrea